Letterlocking

Advance Praise

"*Letterlocking* arrives as dispatches from the interior: singing with secrets and intimacies, eavesdropping on possibility. Daring and unexpected, these poems are letters you will keep and return to often."
—Ruth Awad, author of *Set to Music a Wildfire*

"To friends and enemies, Staab writes, 'I hope [this letter] finds you changed'—a gift she also offers her reader. Encased in *Letterlocking*'s envelopes and coffrets are quiet intimacies, cockroaches, 'blood and melon juice on the counter.' Read these poems like love letters. Read them like secrets."
—Hannah V. Warren, author of *Slaughterhouse for Old Wives' Tales*

Letterlocking

POEMS

STEPHANIE STAAB

Alternating Current Press
Boulder, Colorado

Library of Congress Control Number: 2023943666
ISBN-13 (paperback): 978-1-946580-39-9
ISBN-10 (paperback): 1-946580-39-2
ISBN-13 (ebook): 978-1-946580-40-5

Interior and cover design: Leah Angstman
Cover artwork: "Portrait de Melchior von Brauweiler" by Jan Stephan van Calcar, Venice, 1540
Author photo: Allison Mazur © 2023

Printed in the United States of America
10 9 8 7 6 5 4 3 2 1

Table of Contents

For Susan

Letterlocking

/ˈledər läkiNG/

noun

The traditional technique of folding and securing a written message using small slits, tabs, and holes placed directly into the paper so that no envelope is required and the text cannot be read without breaking the seal, thus providing a secure way to transmit secret messages.

Letters to friends and enemies

I now sit down to let you know
how I get along:
I am well and hope these lines find you
the same.

I hope these lines find you
at the mailbox
savagely ripping open the seal,
dying to know the news.

I hope this letter is served to you on a
silver platter
by a servant interrupting the saddest
dinner party in the world.

I hope this letter finds you in a suburban
bathrobe waiting for the family shower
to be free, listening to Cowboy Junkies
in the yellow kitchen.

I hope it finds you dreamy, reminiscing
about tongues of talented ex-lovers.

I hope this letter finds you crying at the
sink, turned away from the room,
hands floundering in warm, sudsy water.

I hope it finds you changed, altered
like in the hours and days after the Mah-
ler concert.
Quieter.

I hope this letter finds you chastened
and sober
the morning after a drunken fight where
you slapped your only daughter.

I hope it finds you dehydrated.
I hope it finds you among kin.

I hope it is pink-packed snug among
a thousand layers of white business en-
velopes. Fraternizing.

I hope it sails across the sea in a crate
on the slowest, most exquisite container
ship

piloted by a skeleton crew of fourteen
who exchange only a few cursory

but heartfelt
words a day.

> *A photograph is a secret
> about a secret.*
> —Diane Arbus

I have this secret, see,
and you know it too.

It's a small secret:
a dog twitching in her sleep.

We only discuss it between 2 and 5 a.m.
in the parking lot behind the church.

Sometimes, when I tell you the secret
again, you act surprised
as if it were the first time you'd heard
such a thing.

But sometimes you say *yes, yes, I know
that.*

We smile at each other
from across the room
when someone broaches a certain
secret subject.

If we've had too many drinks,
you tell a grim secret to me
but in the morning you don't remember.

Then, I have a double secret:
your secret and the fact that I know it,
that's another one.

It takes a few tries.

Sometimes it's old:
I'm in the cloakroom with my brother's
best friend. The floor smells like cereal.
He doesn't look me in the eye as he tells
me something he's never told anyone. In
the hallway together afterward, my broth-
er pushes him against a wall and says
what were you doing in there with her? (The
crime is always intimacy.)

Sometimes it doesn't matter:
a stranger's grocery list found in the
pages of a library book.

Sometimes it's brutal:
a sniper view of a couple
on the street below,
the woman tucking the man
into her trench coat.

Sermon

I grew up on a boat. The dog fell in the water and someone had to jump in after her.

I grew up on a country estate with its own library. A fainting couch. A humidor. There was a whole room just for chilling bottles of Moët and Pouilly-Fuissé.

I grew up in a log cabin with a tiny baby deer as a pet. I fed her with a bottle and she survived three days in my bedroom.

I grew up on an island; the family owned a hotel. We had great disdain for anyone who wasn't born there. Even those who married an islander were never good enough.

I grew up without brothers and sisters.

I grew up with a distant aunt in the next state who turned out to be my mother.

I grew up with an au pair who mispronounced my name. I loved the way she rearranged me.

I grew up in a building full of cockroaches. People are shocked when I say this, but: They never really bothered me that much.

I grew up with a father who smoked cigars in our swimming pool, idling in the corner on summer nights like Jabba the Hutt.

I grew up in an apartment thick with cigarette smoke. I couldn't take a deep breath until I left the county.

I grew up in a one-room cottage; the family slept all together on mats. Where did my siblings come from?

I grew up with three fathers. One shaved his mustache and I never forgave him, never looked him in the eye again.

I grew up in a house full of pornography. Under every mattress, in every drawer. I wasn't looking for it.

I grew up in seven countries, diplomat parents. My first word was in Mandarin.

I grew up writing letters; we never had a telephone.

I grew up in a church community. Sin was an everyday matter, like chopping vegetables. Jesus was a character in the school play.

You pry and ask questions as if you weren't right there.

I grew up in a house where no one touched each other yet every night we showed up for dinner, waiting for some-one to pull the trigger.

In Grand Central Station, you wait for a train and wish for a hat

With a matching suitcase

like it's 1933
and you're being shipped upstate
to a boarding school
for wayward city girls

like Ella Fitzgerald, her bucolic punish-
ment, her written plan
to run away. Dance shoes and bus fare.

Or maybe you sit at the oyster bar after
work, waiting for your mother.
She shows up late in a sable and asks a
stranger for a cigarette.

Curls of smoke muddle the starry ceil-
ing.
High heels hurt your ankles

but you'd never pay for a taxi. Maybe as
a young woman
you'd put some smell-good on your
pulse points

and walk through the city late at night.
What did you care? What was the point
of a fixed address?

Perhaps your private wish is to catch the
5:23 p.m.
and descend at Spuyten Duyvil in a rum-
pled suit.

To walk into a house with a staircase, a
wooden banister.
To leaf through a delicate stack of mail,
enchanted by handwriting.

To decant amber, fingers pressed against
grooves of crystal cut glass.
Then, a sip and a sigh.

Suspicion

When the woman who lived upstairs knocked on my friend's door and told him his car was on fire, they both walked over to the window together to confirm, a silent and strange moment since they had never spoken before and he hadn't had a woman alone in his apartment for ages and then the police were suddenly there taking details for the report so neither exchanged much personal information or pleasantries and yet in the weeks that followed after the car was towed, after the insurance claim paid out, after he had bought a red Vespa and zipped around dark corners in town, something about their shared-secret smiles in the hallway led him to slide a crisp, tri-folded note under her door one morning, which led to a night together doing clay face masks in her tiny bathroom, a relationship, an elegant wedding on the Cape, a house, a brindle bulldog, a son with red hair, and now in their second decade together, my friend and I sit on the porch with ice in our old-man Scotch whiskies and he asks me quietly and for the first time if I think it's possible she set the car on fire just so she could talk to him.

Spem in Alium

My love worked in the contagious hospi-
tal during the plague.
We were separated by a border;
we wrote letters.

The only news I had to offer
is that I found verbena
growing along the river wall.

That I found it was prescribed to poets
as a tea to cure writers' block
and some say it was used to stanch the
wounds of Jesus.

Most days, I write something useless
like the smell of apple mint drives me
crazy with jealousy.

He, on the other hand, writes of a mira-
cle performed unto him:

Though he touched the faces of the in-
firm
and washed their bodies,

clothed and unclothed them,
he never got sick himself.

Skeptical of miracles, he writes "Spem in
Alium"
on the back of the envelope.

Meaning "Hope in any other."
Meaning "I have never put my hope in
any other than thee."

A mercy.

He asks me to marry him
when this is all

over.

Le coffret de courtoisie

*In Alsace, in the 18th and 19th centuries,
young men would give a "coffret de courtoi-
sie," or a love chest, to their beloved before the
wedding day. She used it to store her jewelry,
ribbons, correspondence, and other small, pre-
cious items.* [1]

Yes, he gave me one
for garlands and silks and billets-doux.

A chest carved with a local talisman: le
grand hamster d'Alsace
and painted with silvery trout from lac
du Forlet
beeches birches pine
chamois boar

But I filled it with snails and earthworms
chocolate-covered cherries I saved and
never ate, blood-sweet
A square of fabric cut from a stranger's
hem in church

Slugs and mushrooms and coal nuggets,
many-winged insects I couldn't identify
doctor's prescriptions I never filled, a
map to what I buried in the remembered
field
an expensive-seeming oil I stole and
rubbed under my eyes, a scheme (writ-
ten and crumpled) to go over a waterfall
in a barrel

A trail sign, a cough.

Lace unravels
and I don't want to be touched
like a cactus.

He and I were not born on the same con-
tinent.
The veil is embroidered in someone
else's tradition.

Love letters cover the desk
in my dreadful handwriting, on scraps
and napkins
but it's never love I am talking about.

That feeling boiled out of me. Definite
like a small bird.

---

1. *from a plaque at the Musée Unterlinden in Colmar, France*

The quilted multiverse

The quilted multiverse theory postulates that every possible event is occurring infinitely many times in nature, thus there are infinitely many universes resembling ours.

—Frontiers in Physics journal

One way, you pass a house with chickens in the yard and you think, "Ah, I've always wanted chickens. I'd be better with chickens."

One way, you go everywhere by bike and live in a flap tent alone. Your thighs are sculpted like marble.

One way, you work as a mailman, fulfilling a gnawing dream from childhood, openly reading postcards on the sidewalk.

One way is full of bubbles: bathtubs, gum, champagne, hot springs.

One way, you live over water. A Mississippi riverboat gambler or a Breton oyster farmer.

One way is very short but satisfying. Like a sneeze or an orgasm.

One way is a wrong turn and you can see the straight path in the valley below but it's impossible to reach it on foot.

One way is dark, full of witchcraft and mistakes.

One way brings you through a portal to another dimension where all this, the virus, never happened and you go on overnight train journeys in sleeper cars and kiss and touch strangers, their alien eyebrows different than yours.

There is, of course, a parallel universe
where your hand slips
slicing this bright cantaloupe.
Blood and melon juice on the counter.
Nine-fingered for the rest of your days.

Bless, it already happened.

A LITTLE
PIGEON BOOK

About the Author

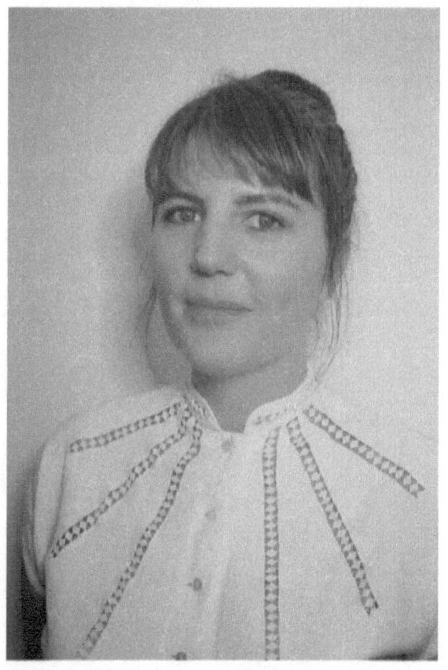

Stephanie Staab is an American poet living in the Black Forest, Germany. Her work has appeared in *Gulf Coast*, *Lake Effect*, *Lunch Ticket*, *Chestnut Review*, and *Ligeia Magazine*, among other outlets.

Acknowledgments

Many thanks to the editors of these publications where the following poems first appeared:

Ligeia Magazine: "Letters to friends and enemies"

The Summerset Review: "[I have this secret, see,]"

Crab Creek Review: "Sermon"

Chiron Review: "Suspicion"

Lunch Ticket: "The quilted multiverse"

Author Thanks

Thank you to my friends for the bonhomie during the creation of this book: Laura Hughes, Eiren Shea, Julia Tadlock, Emily Thetford-Smith, Allison Mazur, Danielle Hillebrecht, Ed Baker, Raphael Bob-Waksberg, Matt Wellins, Hannah V. Warren, Anne Shoemaker, Melissa Parsons, Colleen Rober, Helen Shannon.

I am very grateful to the members of the Freiburg Writers' Group, for providing a warm literary community in a place where, for many years, I had none.

All my love and a French kiss to Gaëtan Meissner: *Jusqu'au centième année.*

Most of all, thanks to my mother, Susan Valerie Hornyak Staab, who taught me the ways of the epistolary life.

Colophon

The edition you are holding is the First Edition of this publication.

The handwritten title font is set in Fighter, created by Olex Studio. The secondary cover font is set in 1550, created by Frédéric Michaud. The tertiary serif cover font is set in Century, created by Morris Fuller Benton. The Alternating Current Press logo is set in Portmanteau, created by JLH Fonts. The page numbers are set in Avenir Book, created by Adrian Frutiger. All other text is set in Iowan Old Style, created by John Downer. All fonts used with permission and full commercial license; all rights reserved.

LITTLE
PIGEON
SERIES

altcurrentpress.com

www.ingramcontent.com/pod-product-compliance
Lightning Source LLC
Chambersburg PA
CBHW030847200726
48285CB00007B/2578